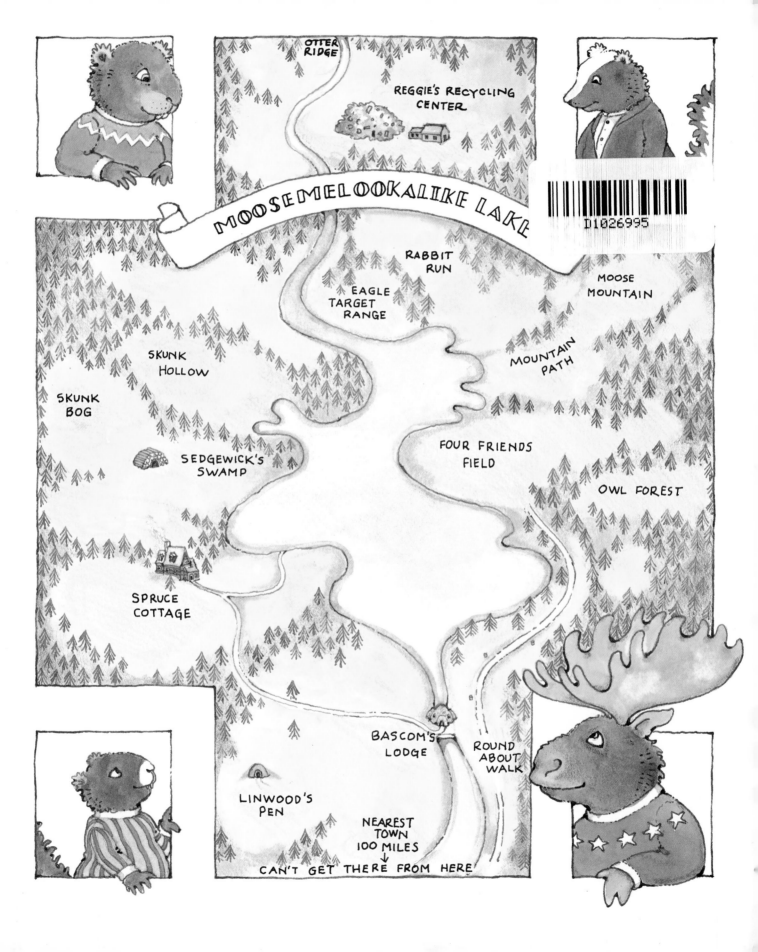

Sarah Stapler

Spruce the Moose
Cuts Loose

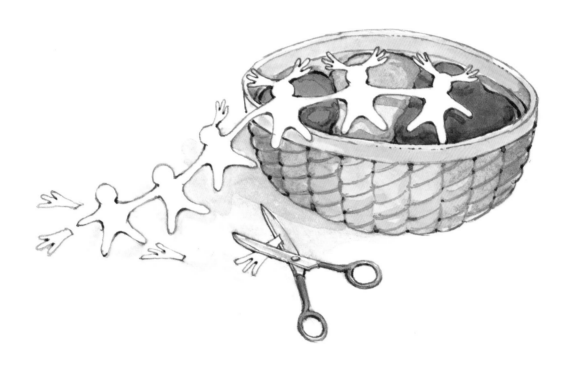

Troll Associates

For Dorothy Waldo Stapler

Text and illustrations copyright © 1992 by Sarah Stapler
G. P. Putnam's Sons, a division of The Putnam & Grosset Book Group,
200 Madison Avenue, New York, NY 10016.
Published simultaneously in Canada.
Printed in USA.
Book design by Jean Weiss
The text is set in Caxton Light

Library of Congress Cataloging-in-Publication Data
Stapler, Sarah
Spruce the Moose cuts loose / by Sarah Stapler.
p. cm.
Summary: Spruce the moose's enormous antlers
cause him all sorts of problems in his daily life.
[1. Moose—Fiction. 2. Animals—Fiction.] I. Title.
PZ7.S7934Sp   1992
[E]—dc20
90-23105 CIP AC
ISBN 0-399-21861-0
1 3 5 7 9 10 8 6 4 2
First Impression

$\mathbf{E}$very year Spruce's antlers grew longer and longer until midwinter, when they fell off. But this year, midwinter had gone by with his antlers still growing.

"This is ridiculous," Spruce sighed as he stared at his bedroom ceiling. "They've grown so large that I can't even sleep."

The week started out awful and got worse. Spruce's antlers got in the way everywhere he went. On Monday, he got stuck in the bathroom door and spent an hour getting loose.

"I hate antlers," he grumbled.

On Tuesday, hanging up his laundry, he came up under the clothesline the wrong way.

"Oh, not again," he said, frowning.

On Wednesday, Spruce tried to fill the feeders, but it didn't work.
"This is so embarrassing," he mumbled as a bird landed on his
nose. "Shoo!"

And on Thursday, he really ran into trouble. Carting his wood home, Spruce made the mistake of taking the shortcut under the big fir tree.

"Help, help!" he yelled, until his friends Bascom, Sedgewick, and Linwood heard him.

"Never fear, Spruce. Help is here!" Bascom said, and then he cut the fir branch down.

"I hate antlers!" Spruce shouted after the branch fell on his head.

"But, Spruce, your antlers are wonderful. They make you look majestic," Bascom said.

"I would much prefer antlers to this bushy tail of mine," added Sedgewick.

"I've always wanted antlers too," chimed in Linwood.

Spruce didn't believe them. That night he tossed and turned, wondering what could go wrong next.

Then Spruce remembered, "It's Bascom's birthday tomorrow."

Spruce checked his jelly cabinet for the miniature birch-bark canoe he had made Bascom last summer.

"Ah, it's there. It's wrapped!" Spruce smiled for the first time in a long while.

The next day Spruce went about his business. He chopped
wood, shoveled snow, and made muffins.

"Hurray!" he sang. "I've made it through the day without getting stuck in a door or a tree."

When it was time to go to the birthday party, he went to the jelly cupboard to get Bascom's present.

"Oh, no!" cried Spruce. "I can't reach it!" He tried everything. He turned his head to the side. He wiggled on his back and used his feet. He even tried snatching the present with a broom, but all he did was break half of his jelly jars.

Spruce called Linwood and Sedgewick, but they had already left.

"It's too late to make a new present. I'm already late for the party," Spruce thought. So he picked up the first thing that he saw—the old battered muffin tin that he had made muffins in earlier—and he stuck it in a paper bag.

"I have to give Bascom something," he cried.

When Spruce arrived at Bascom's lodge, Sedgewick and Linwood were already there. Sedgewick handed Bascom a large, beautifully wrapped box.

"I hope you like it," he said as Bascom carefully unwrapped the gift.

"Oh!" Bascom smiled broadly. "It's a bird feeder. I love it."
Bascom opened Linwood's present next.

"A periscope! I've always wanted a periscope. Thank you, Linwood."

Bascom looked at Spruce and the muffin-tin bag.

"Oh, this bag," stammered Spruce. "This is just something that I carry around with me. I think I left your present in the other room. I'll go and look for it."

Spruce backed up into the next room. He didn't get very far.

"I'm stuck!" he cried.

His friends pulled and prodded, but they could not get him loose.

Spruce dropped his bag and the muffin tin fell out.

"Why do you carry a messy muffin tin around with you?" asked Sedgewick.

Spruce was so upset that he told them the truth about the real present, his antlers, the jelly cupboard, and the awful week he'd had.

"And now I've ruined Bascom's birthday party," he added.

Bascom said, "You silly moose. You don't have to worry about my present. You haven't ruined my party." Then Bascom, Linwood, and Sedgewick gave Spruce a huge hug. Just as they hugged him, Spruce felt something snap.

"Look!" Sedgewick yelled. "Spruce has lost his antlers."

"Hurray! Hurray! I've finally lost my antlers," Spruce shouted.
Then he ran back, pulled the antlers loose, and presented them
to Bascom.

"Happy birthday, Bascom," he chortled.

"Spruce, what a wonderful present. I've always wanted a pair
of antlers," Bascom said.

Then they found a hammer and some nails, and hung the antlers over the door.

Finally, Sedgewick and Linwood set Bascom's table with the party things and brought in Bascom's birthday cake. They sang "Happy Birthday" and helped Bascom wish. Then everyone had an extra-big slice.